Lunchbox Jokes, Food: 100 Fun Tear-Out Notes for Kids
by Deana Gunn and Wona Miniati
Designed by Lilla Hangay

Published by Brown Bag Publishers, LLC
P.O. Box 235065
Encinitas, CA 92023
www.lunchbox-jokes.com

Printed in China by Overseas Printing Corp.

ISBN   978-1-938706-15-8

How to Use Lunchbox Jokes:

This book contains 100 tear-out notes, each with a joke. Simply tear out one note, fold it in half (with the question on the outside and the punch line on the inside), and place in your child's lunchbox.

Fold!

Why did the chicken cross the road?

To get to the other side!

These ready-made notes are easy to use and a great way to brighten lunchtime. Kids can enjoy the joke, read it out loud, or pass the fun along to a friend.

Even shy kids love to read jokes out loud and share laughs all around the table.

Don't be surprised to hear one at dinner – kids like to see if mom and dad can guess the punch line too!

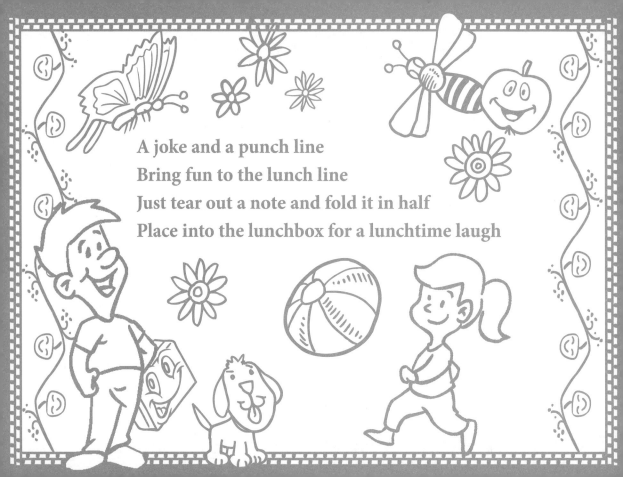

A joke and a punch line
Bring fun to the lunch line
Just tear out a note and fold it in half
Place into the lunchbox for a lunchtime laugh

What did
one plate
say to
the other
plate?

Lunch is
on me!

What do potatoes wear to bed?

Their yammies

Why did the tomato blush?

Because
it saw
the salad
dressing

How do
you make
a fruit
punch?

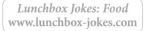

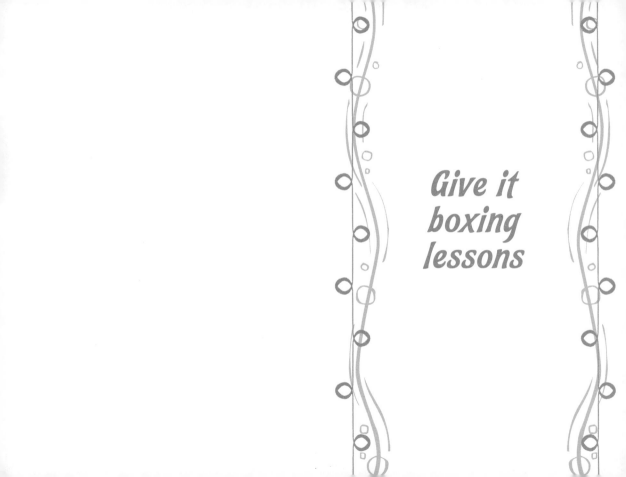

Give it boxing lessons

What do you call a sheep that is covered in chocolate?

A Hershey baaaaar

What does
a snowman
eat for
breakfast?

Frosted
flakes

How
do you
make
an
egg
roll?

Push it

How do you
fix a broken
pizza?

With
tomato
paste

What did
the chef
say to the
mushroom?

You are a
fun-guy

What is a
tree's favorite
drink?

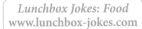

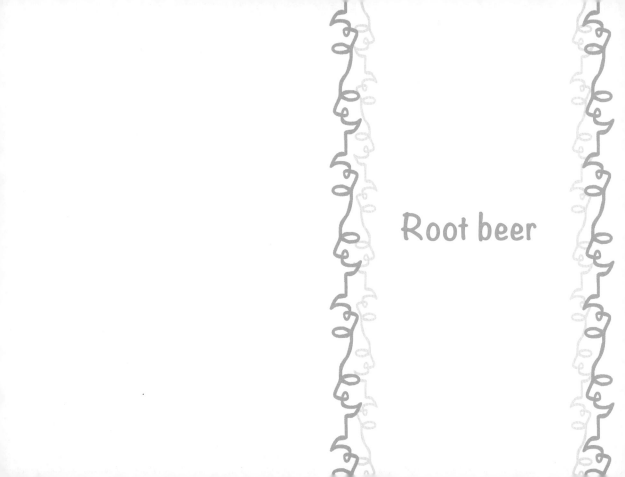

Root beer

Why did the chef have to chase after his breakfast?

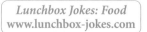

Because
the eggs
were runny

What do they serve in the salvage yard cafeteria?

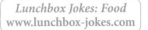

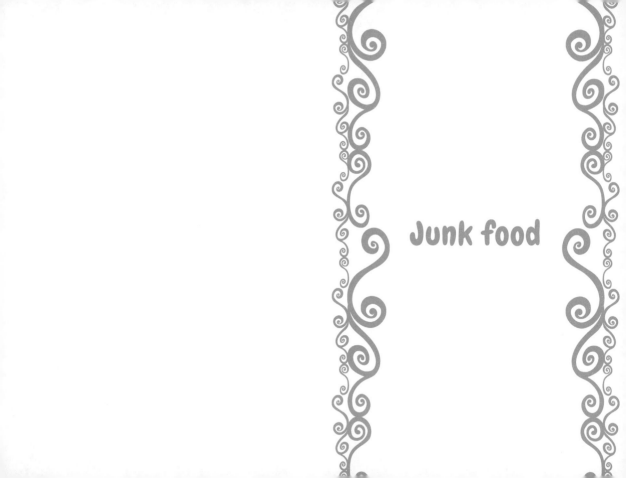

Junk food

Why did the baseball player throw pancakes in the stands?

Because the
umpire said
"Batter up!"

What do you call a car made of orange rinds?

An automo-peel

Why were the baby strawberries upset?

Their mom
and dad were
in a jam

What candy
do you
eat on the
playground?

Recess pieces

What do
you call a
peanut in a
spacesuit?

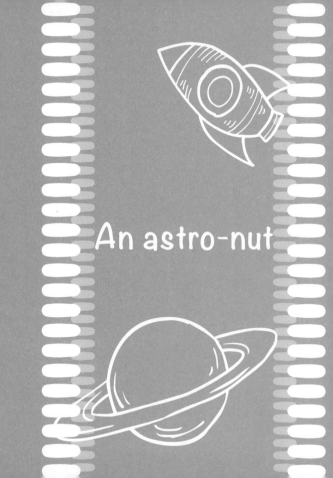

An astro-nut

What kind of fish goes best with peanut butter?

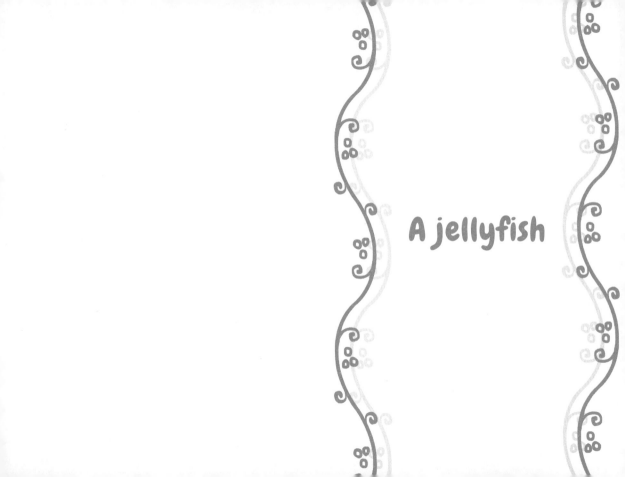

A jellyfish

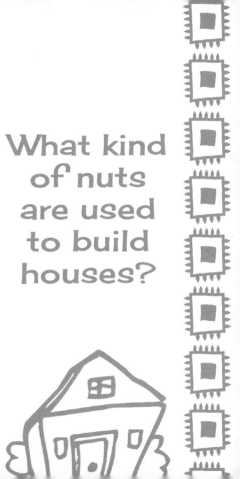

What kind
of nuts
are used
to build
houses?

What did the chewing gum say to the shoe?

I'm stuck
on you!

What do you call a train carrying a load of bubble gum?

A chew–chew train

What kind of keys do kids like to carry?

Cookies

What do
you give
a sick
lemon?

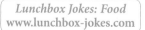

Lemon
aid

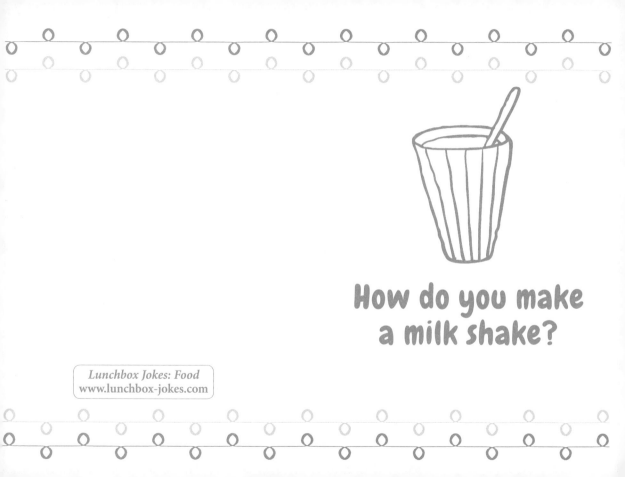

How do you make
a milk shake?

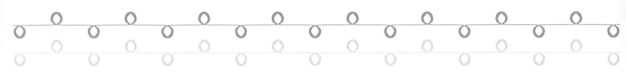

Give it
a good
scare

Why shouldn't you tell a secret on a farm?

Lunchbox Jokes: Food
www.lunchbox-jokes.com

Because the potatoes have eyes and the corn has ears

What kind of
nuts always
seem to have
a cold?

Cashews

What is a ghost's favorite food?

Spook-getti

Why did the
boy eat his
homework?

The teacher
said it was a
piece of cake

What do you call cheese that's not yours?

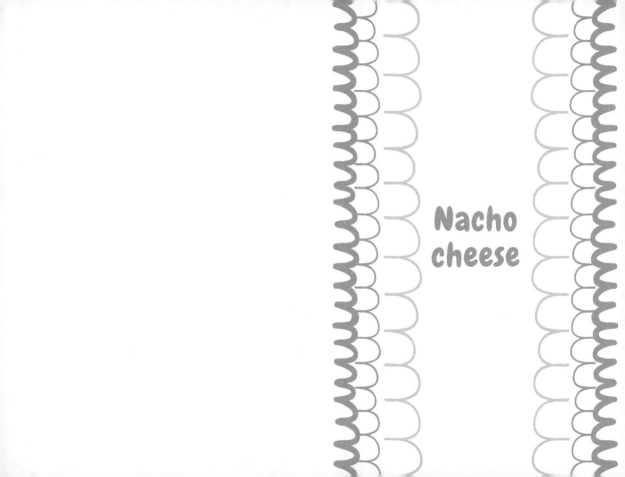

Nacho cheese

What do
skeletons
say
before
they eat?

Bone appetit

What did the salad say before dinner?

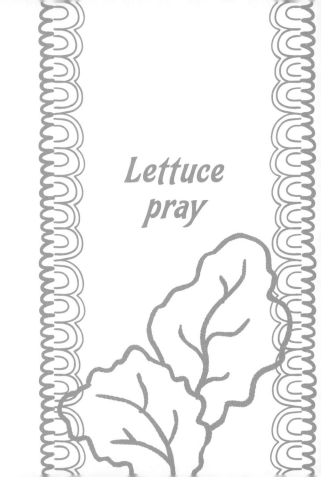

Lettuce pray

What do you call a sad strawberry?

A blueberry

When do
you go on
red and stop
on green?

When you're
eating a
watermelon

What is
an alien's
favorite
sweet
treat?

Martian-mallows

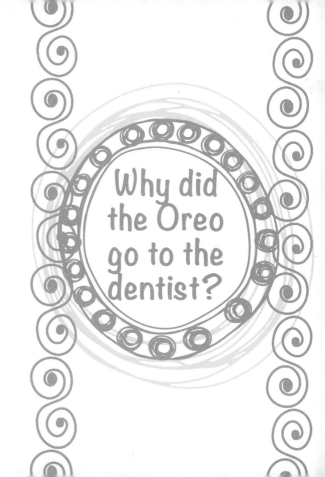

Why did the Oreo go to the dentist?

Because
he lost his
filling

Where do
burgers like
to dance?

At the
meat ball

How do you make a cucumber laugh?

Pickle it!

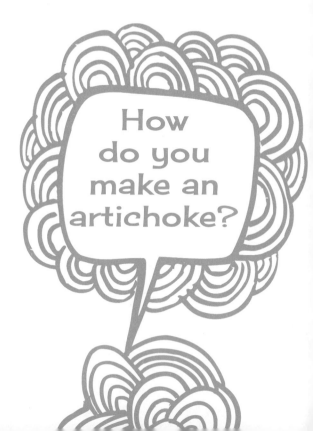

How do you make an artichoke?

Why aren't
bananas
ever
lonely?

Because
they come
in bunches

What
did the
hamburger
say to
the dill
pickle?

You're
dill-icious!

Knock, knock!
Who's there?
Olive.
Olive who?

What do
you call a
fast fungi?

A mush-vroom

How did
the pea
feel when
he was in a
bad mood?

Lunchbox Jokes: Food
www.lunchbox-jokes.com

Grum-pea

What do you get when you cross a pig with a millipede?

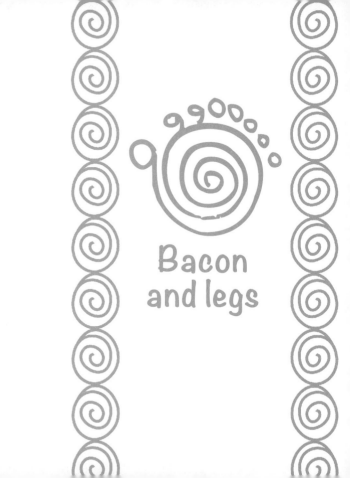

Bacon
and legs

What's the worst vegetable to serve on a boat?

Leeks

What kind
of jokes do
vegetables
tell?

Corny
jokes

If fruit comes from a fruit tree, what kind of tree does chicken come from?

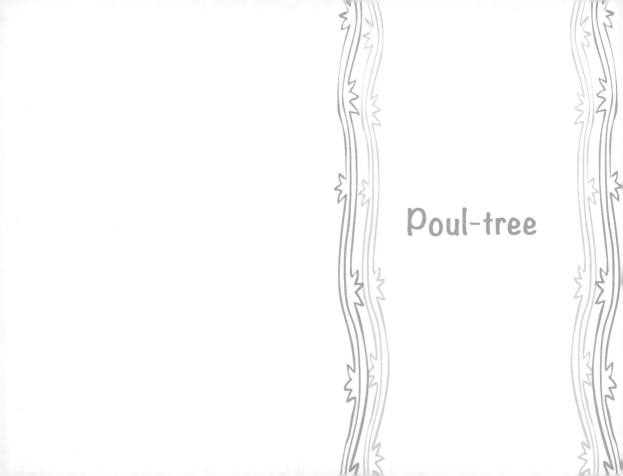

Poul-tree

Why did
the baker
stop making
donuts?

He was
tired of
the hole
thing

What
do little
vampires
eat?

Alpha-bat
soup

Knock knock!
Who's there?
Lettuce.
Lettuce who?

Lettuce in
and you'll
find out!

What do witches put on their bagels?

Scream cheese

What do you get when you cross dessert with a snake?

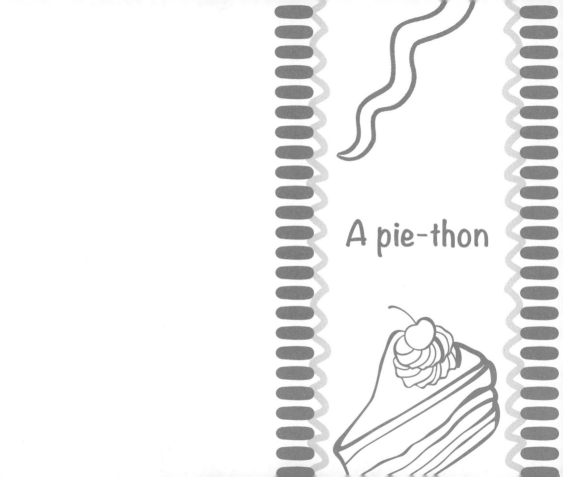

A pie-thon

What are
the tastiest
days of the
week?

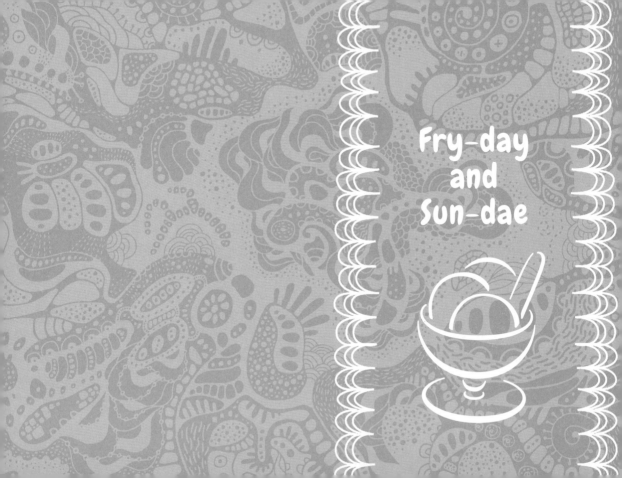

Fry-day
and
Sun-dae

Knock knock!
Who's there?
Orange.
Orange who?

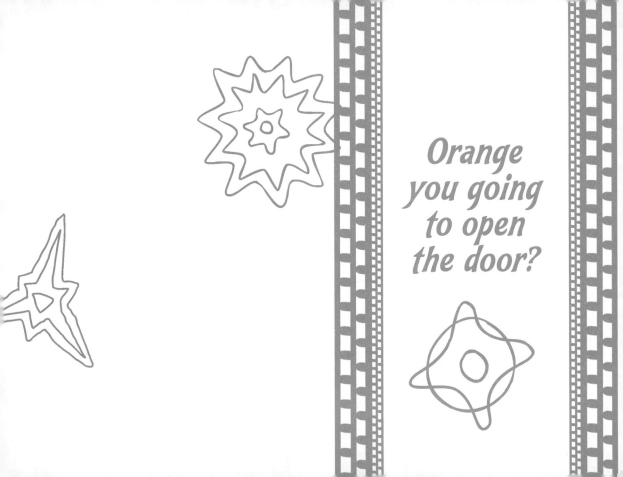

Orange you going to open the door?

What did the slow tomato say to the fast tomato?

What is Luke Skywalker's least favorite vegetable?

Darth
Tater

What did the mother ghost say to the baby ghost when it ate too fast?

*Stop
goblin
your
food!*

What
does the
astronaut
use to eat
his food?

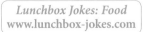

Satellite
dishes

Why shouldn't you tell secrets in a cornfield?

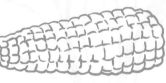

There are
too many
ears

What do
you call
a rich
melon?

A melon-aire

How does a lemon ask for a hug?

"Give me a squeeze!"

Why did the
man eat his
lunch at the
bank?

Lunchbox Jokes: Food
www.lunchbox-jokes.com

He
wanted to
eat rich
food

What do chickens grow on?

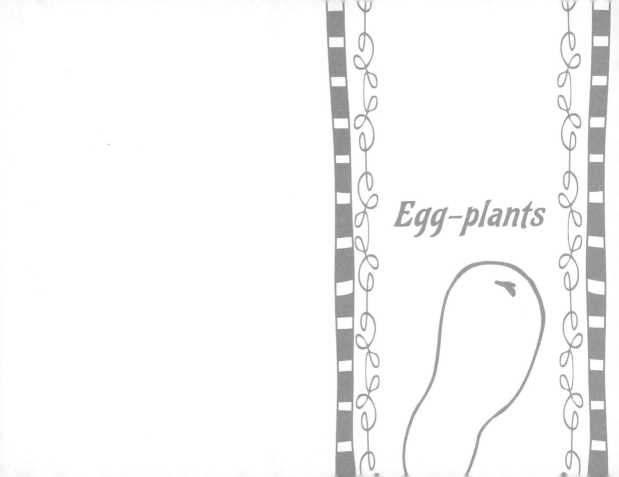

Egg-plants

Why don't
eggs tell
jokes?

Because they'd crack each other up

What
did one
snowman
say to
another?

Everything
smells like
carrots
to me

When is an
apple a
grouch?

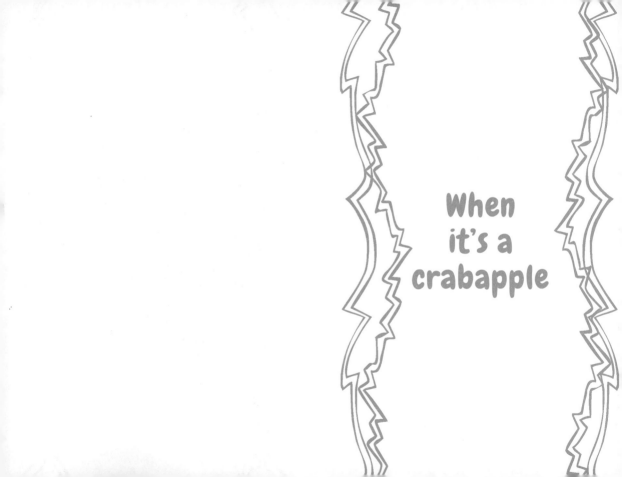

When
it's a
crabapple

What kinds of shoes are made from banana peels?

Slippers

What
vegetable
can you
sew with?

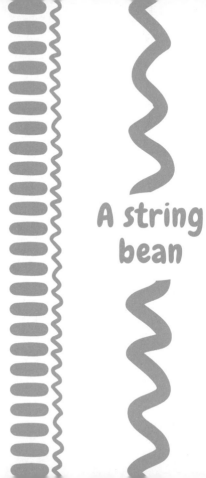

A string
bean

What kind of an apple is not an apple?

A pineapple

How
do you
make
gold
soup?

Add 24
carrots

What vegetable
do you get when
you cross a dog
with a flower?

A collie-
flower

Why did
the donut
go to the
dentist?

So it could get a chocolate filling

Why did the bean fall in love with the tortilla?

It was
burritoful

What kind of potatoes do they serve on the Death Star?

Vader Tots

Why did the vegetables want to dance?

Because the
music had a
good beet

How do you make a strawberry shake?

What is a gorilla's favorite food?

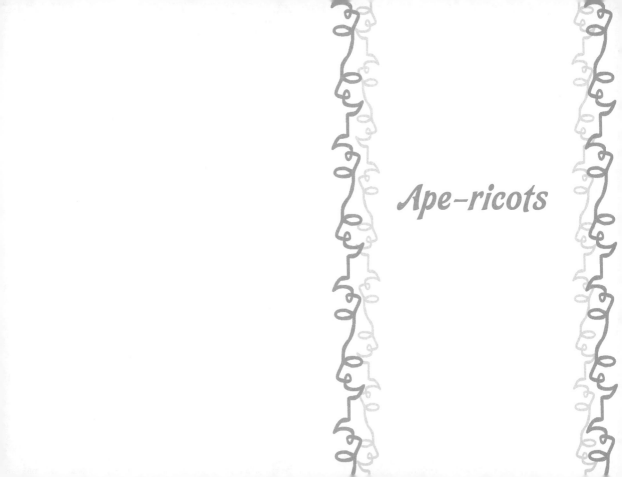

Ape-ricots

What kind of vegetable is found in the basement?

Lunchbox Jokes: Food
www.lunchbox-jokes.com

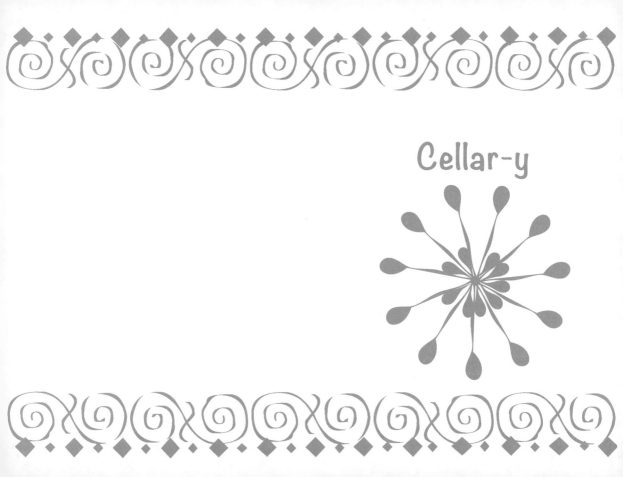

Cellar-y

What is a
vampire's
favorite
fruit?

A neck-
tarine

What school subject is full of fruit?

*History –
because it
has a lot
of dates*

What fruit teases you a lot?

Ba-na-na-
na-na-na!

How do you fix a broken pumpkin?

With a
pumpkin
patch

What is
green
and
goes to
summer
camp?

A
Brussels
scout

Where were
potatoes first
fried?

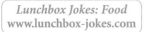

In Greece

What do
you use
to open a
banana?

A mon-key

What do you call an apple that plays the trumpet?

A tooty
fruity

?

Knock,
knock!
Who's there?
Figs
Figs who?

Figs the
doorbell,
it's
broken.